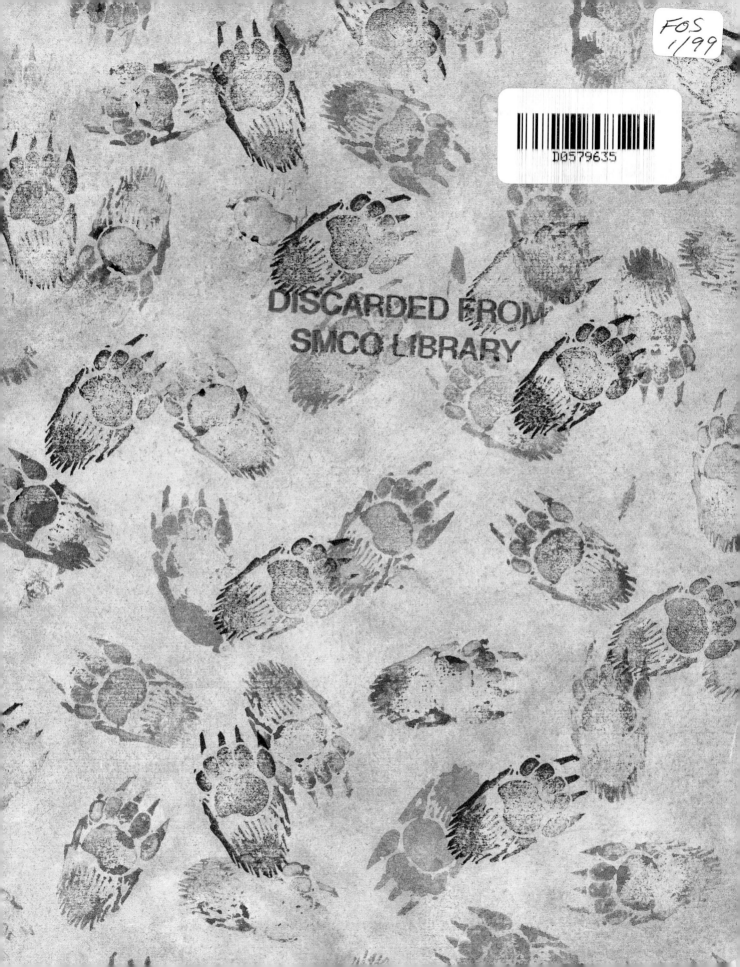

Library of Congress Cataloging-in-Publication Data

Schubert, Ingrid, 1953-
    [Lieber Heinrich. English]
    There's a hole in my bucket / Ingrid & Dieter Schubert.
       p. cm.
    Summary: A retelling of a German folksong about a bear unable to
water his flowers because every attempt to repair the hole in his bucket
only leads to further problems.
    ISBN 1-886910-28-6 (alk. paper)
    [1. Folklore—Germany.] I. Schubert, Dieter, 1947-
II. Title.
PZ8.1.S375L1 1998
398.2'0943'0452978—dc21
[E]   97-39086

Ingrid and Dieter Schubert

There's a Hole in My Bucket

Front Street & Lemniscaat

Asheville, North Carolina

One day the sun was so hot the flowers in front of Bear's hole wilted.

"I have to water them quickly," Bear thought, looking around.
"What can I use to get some water?"

"A spoon? No, too small," he mused.
"A cup? Still too small.

Maybe a strainer? No. Bad idea. But I do have a bucket.
Where is it?"

Bear looked and looked and finally he found his bucket.
It had a hole in it.

"*This* is a problem. What am I going to do now?" he wondered.
Just then Hedgehog came by.

"What's the matter, Bear?"
"My flowers are thirsty and I need to water them.
But there's a hole in my bucket."

"So fix the hole," said Hedgehog.

"With what?"

"With straw. Come on, I'll show you."

Together they gathered straw.
But the blades were too long.
Bear tried to break them, but the straw was too tough.

"You have to cut it," said Hedgehog.—"With what?" Bear asked.
Hedgehog thought. "Wait a minute. I'll run home.
I have just the right thing there."

Bear got down and studied his flowers.
They looked very sad. "Don't let your heads droop,"
Bear said, trying to cheer them up.

Hedgehog came back with a pair of scissors.
"You can cut the straw into small pieces with these."
Bear took the scissors, gleefully.

Snip-snap. Snip-snap.

But the scissors wouldn't cut.

"These are dull," Bear said. "What now?"

"You have to sharpen them," Hedgehog said.

"With what?"

"With a stone, of course," said Hedgehog.

They looked everywhere until, at last, they found a perfect stone

and carried it to Bear's house.

Bear sat down, took the scissors, and tried to sharpen them.
"That's not the way to do it," Hedgehog cried out.
"To sharpen a pair of scissors with a stone you need water."
Bear stroked his chin. "I don't have any water."

"Then go to the lake and get some."
"With what?" — "With a bucket!"
"But there's a hole in my bucket," said Bear.
"Oh," said Hedgehog.

Then it started to rain. At first a few drops, then more and more.
"You can't go home now," Bear said. "Come with me.
My hole is warm and dry. We'll figure this out later."

They sat all afternoon in Bear's hole and had a great time together.

When the rain was over they went outside and guess what?
The flowers didn't droop their heads anymore.
Bear was so happy that he picked a bouquet.

"For you, Hedgehog, because you were such a great help."
"I'll go home right away and put these in water," said Hedgehog.
"Do you have something to put them in?" asked Bear.

"No," Hedgehog said. "Can I borrow your bucket?"

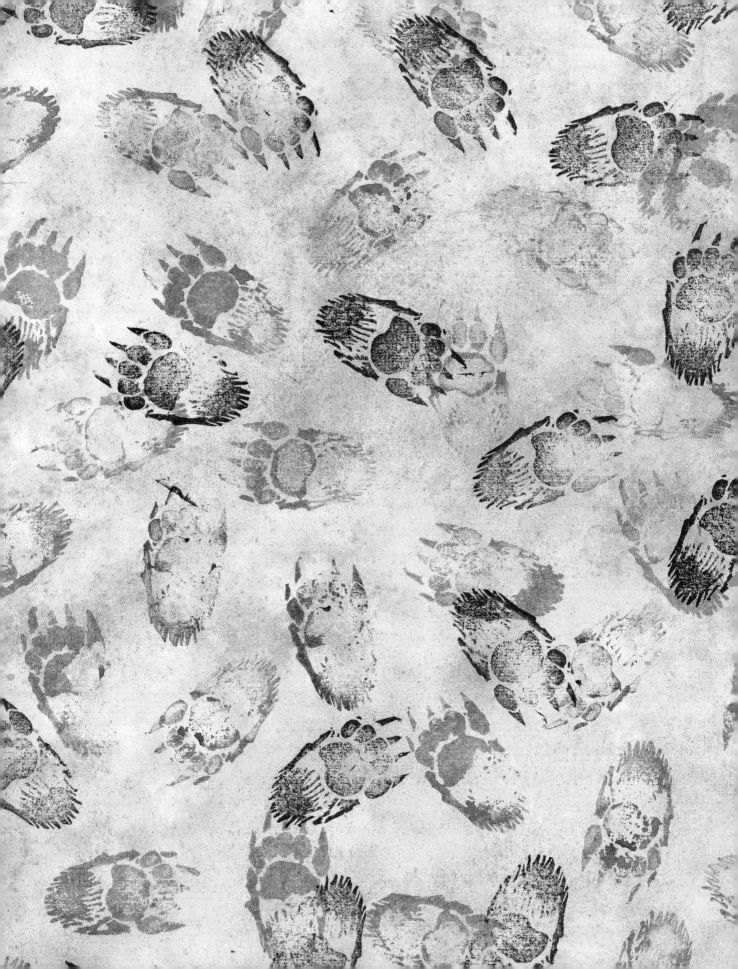